# ROBINSON

## BY PETER SÍS

SCHOLASTIC PRESS / NEW YORK

MY FRIENDS AND I LOVE ADVENTURE.

WE PLAY PIRATES ALL THE TIME. TOGETHER, WE RULE THE HIGH SEAS!

So when the school costume party is announced,
of course we know we will go as pirates.

MY MOM HAS A DIFFERENT IDEA.
"PETER, IF YOU LOVE ADVENTURE, WHY DON'T YOU GO AS
ROBINSON CRUSOE?" SHE SAYS.
"I WANT TO BE A PIRATE WITH MY FRIENDS," I SAY.

"BUT ROBINSON CRUSOE IS THE HERO OF YOUR FAVORITE STORY."
MOM IS RIGHT. HE *WAS* A GREAT ADVENTURER, AND BRAVER THAN
ALL THE PIRATES. "OKAY, I'LL DO IT!" I SAY.
MOM GATHERS MATERIALS, AND I WATCH HER GET TO WORK.

WHEN SHE PUTS ALL THE PIECES TOGETHER — WOW!
I REALLY DO LOOK LIKE ROBINSON CRUSOE.

ON THE WALK TO SCHOOL, I AM BURSTING
WITH EXCITEMENT. WHAT WILL MY FRIENDS SAY?

I can't wait for them to see me!

BUT WHEN THEY DO, THEY LAUGH AND TEASE ME. MY SKIN GROWS HOT. I DON'T FEEL STRONG OR BRAVE ANYMORE.

I WANT TO LEAVE.

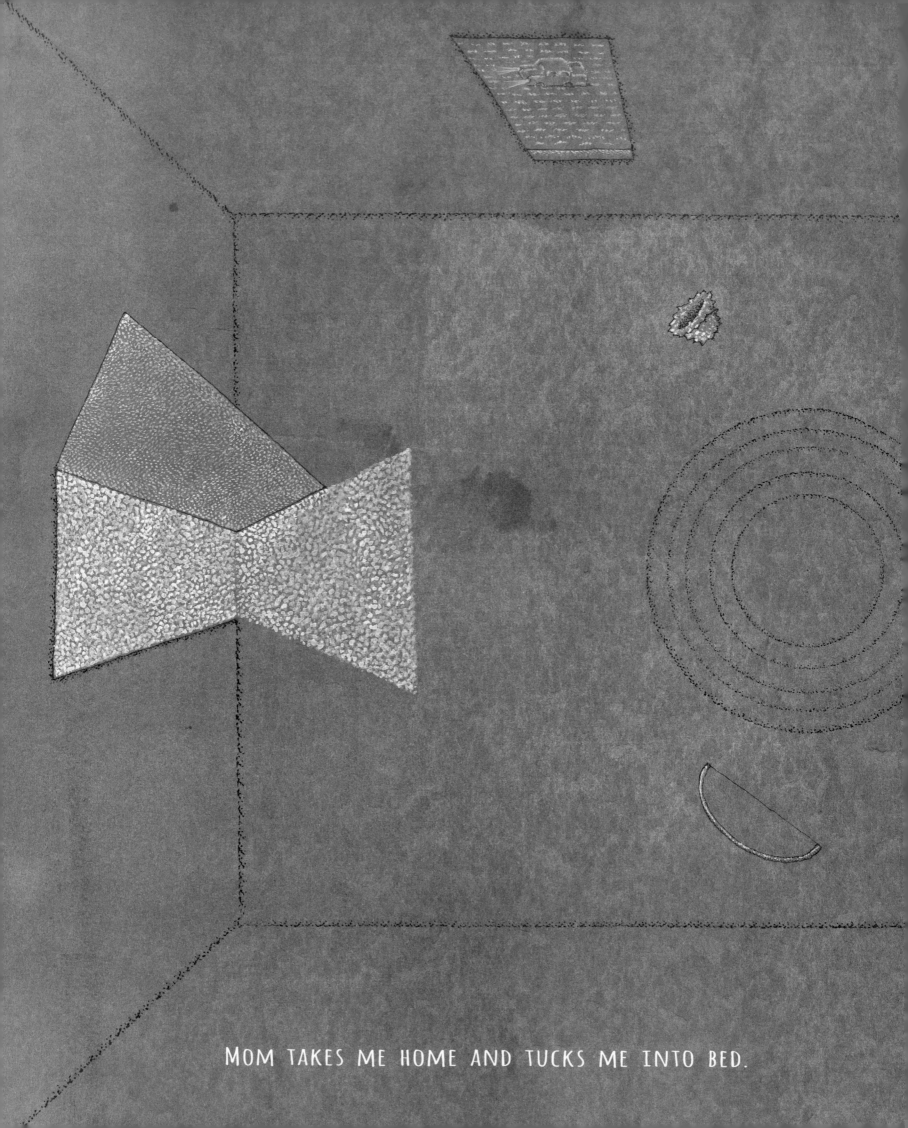

MOM TAKES ME HOME AND TUCKS ME INTO BED.

My head swims.

I TOSS AND TURN.

I FEEL LOST.

I AM DRIFTING.

I FLOAT IN AND OUT OF HOURS, OR MAYBE DAYS,

UNTIL I AM CAST UPON AN ISLAND.

EVERYTHING LOOKS UNFAMILIAR.

IS THERE NO ONE HERE BUT ME?

HOW WILL I SURVIVE ON MY OWN?

I FIND WATER AND
SOMETHING TO EAT.

I BUILD A SHELTER TO PROTECT MYSELF FROM STORMS AND THE HOT SUN.

I FIGURE OUT HOW TO MAKE CLOTHES THAT ARE BETTER FOR LIFE ON AN ISLAND.

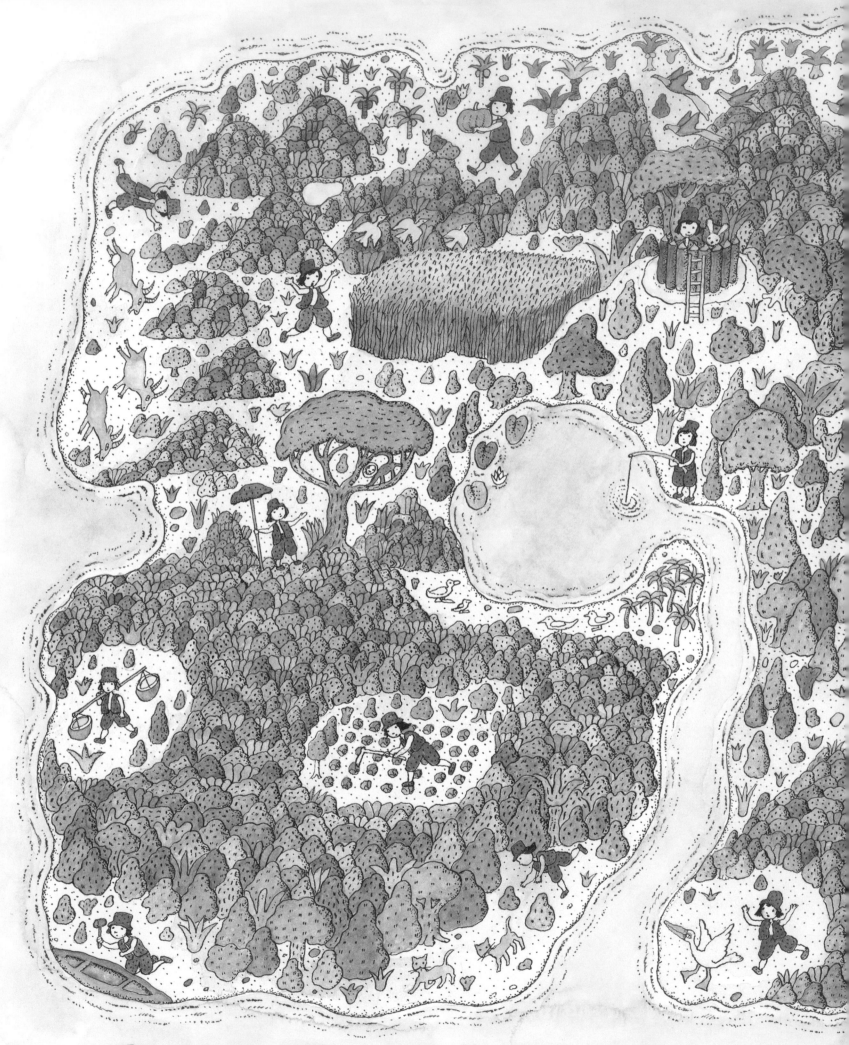

THE ANIMALS HERE ARE KIND. WE BECOME FRIENDS.

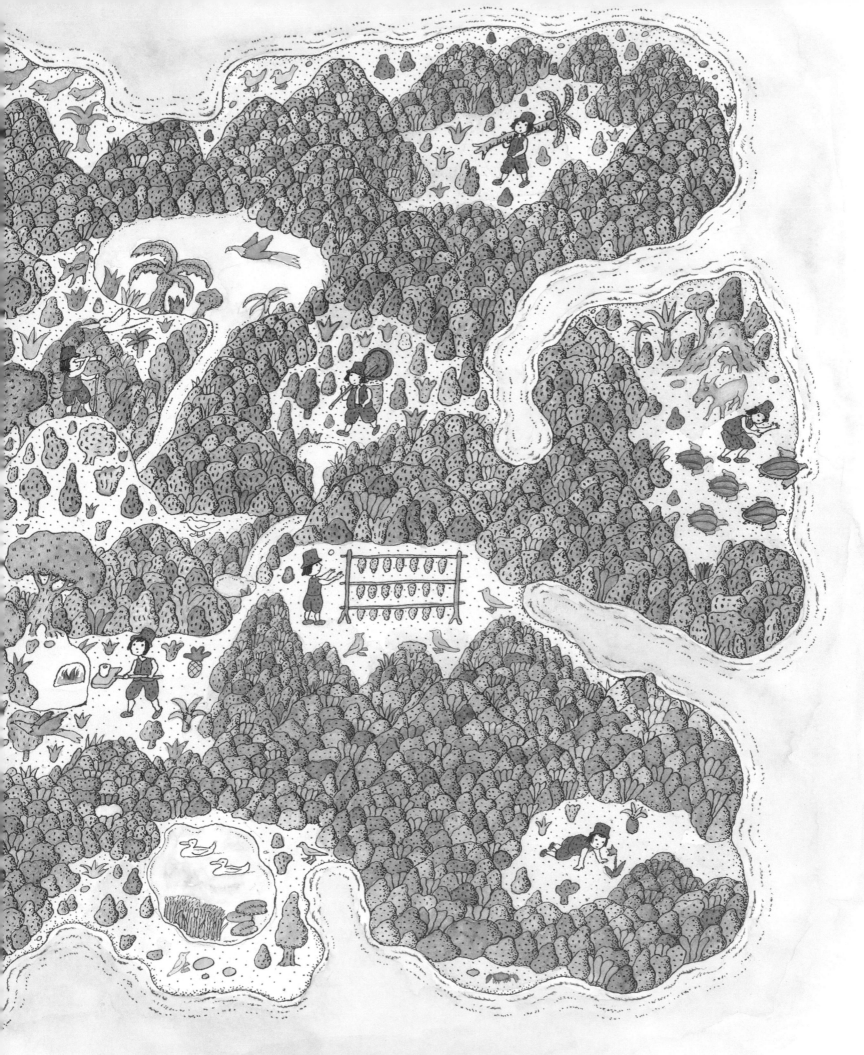

THEY KEEP ME COMPANY WHILE I WORK.

I INVITE THEM TO MY TABLE AND WE CELEBRATE THE HARVEST.

I FEEL STRONGER NOW AND BRAVE.

THE ISLAND IS MY HOME.

BUT I AM ALWAYS ON THE LOOKOUT FOR PIRATES.

THEY ARE HERE . . . !

QUIETLY, I SLIP INTO THE TREES AND HIDE.

HAVE THEY COME TO PLUNDER AND SPOIL?

NO . . . MY FRIENDS WANT TO
PLAY AND HEAR MORE ABOUT
ROBINSON CRUSOE.

I AM HAPPY TO SEE THEM.

And together again, we set off on a new adventure.

# Author's Note

*Robinson Crusoe* by Daniel Defoe, with its magical illustrations, was one of my favorite books as a child. I was enchanted by the fictional story of a shipwrecked castaway who survives on a remote island for many years just by being smart and skilled.

My book, *Robinson*, is inspired by a true story from my boyhood. It came back to me when I found this photo of me dressed up as the brave adventurer for a costume contest at school. My mother, Alenka, who was an artist and good with her hands, made me the costume using my sister's leotard, a vest, a wig, some skins or mini carpets, and faux fur. She also made me a bow and some sort of spear. I won first prize, and my photo appeared on the front page of the local newspaper. My mother was so proud.

But my memory is that I was uncomfortable. The leotard kept slipping. The skins were itchy. My makeup was melting. I could not wait to go home, especially when my friends and all the children made fun of me (clearly, they had not read *Robinson Crusoe*).

I was running a fever and stayed in bed for days. Did I really travel to Crusoe's "Island of Despair"? Whatever happened in those lonely days of my shipwreck, it made me stronger. In my solitude, I became master of my own island. And I believed in myself again. So when my friends came to visit, I was able to forgive and forget and move on. They all wanted to hear stories of Robinson Crusoe, and we may have even read the book together.

My friends and I had a lot of adventures after that, discovering the North Pole and exploring the Himalayas . . . But that just might be another book.

— Peter Sís

FOR MY MOTHER

Copyright © 2017 by Peter Sís

Library of Congress Cataloging-in-Publication Data available
ISBN 978-0-545-73166-9
10 9 8 7 6 5 4 3 2 1          17 18 19 20 21

Printed in China 38
First edition, October 2017
Book design by Charles Kreloff and David Saylor

## ABOUT THE ART

The art for *Robinson* was created using pen, ink, and watercolor. I wanted the pictures, and the process of making them, to be as free as my childhood imagination. The story is a dream after all. I tried to recreate that colorful, dreamlike first impression I had when reading *Robinson Crusoe* as a boy through color, style, and the emotion of each page.